Everyone Makes a Difference

A Story About Community

Written by
Cindy Leaney

Illustrated by
Peter Wilks

Foundations for the
Future Charter Academy

Rourke
Publishing LLC
Vero Beach, Florida 32964

Before you read this story, take a look at the front cover of the book. The boy in the middle is a friend from India.

1. What are all three kids doing?

2. What do you think their activity has to do with the community?

Produced by SGA Illustration and Design
Designed by Phil Kay
Series Editor: Frank Sloan

www.rourkepublishing.com

Library of Congress Cataloging-in-Publication Data

Leaney, Cindy.
    Everyone makes a difference : community / by Cindy Leaney ; illustrated by Peter Wilks.
        p. cm. -- (Hero club character)
    Summary: Matt and Jose help welcome a new young boy from India by introducing him to the activities of the local Community Center.
    ISBN 1-58952-733-X
    [1. Citizenship--Fiction. 2. Interpersonal relations--Fiction. 3. Conduct of life--Fiction.]
    I. Wilks, Peter ill. II. Title.

PZ7.L46335Ev 2003
[E]--dc21

                                                                            2003043232

Printed in the USA
MP/W

Welcome to The Hero Club!

Read about all the things that happen to them.

Try and guess what they'll do next.

www.theheroclub.com

"Kids, this is Vikram. He and his parents just moved here. Vikram's dad works with me at the hospital."

"Hi, Vikram. I'm Matt."

"Hi. My name's José."

"We're going down to the Community Center. Do you want to come with us, Vikram?"

"Okay. What do you do there?"

"Lots of different things."

"What else do you do?"

"We run errands."

"Or we help people in their yards."

"We've got lots of projects."

"Wow, look at that. The kids in that car just threw their junk out in the street."

"That's so dumb."

"Totally dumb."

"Hi!"

"Hi!"

"This is Vikram. He's from India."

"Cool. Are you on vacation?"

14

"No, my father works at the hospital.
We're moving here."

"Excellent."

"Come on, Vikram. I'll show you around. We'll be back in a few minutes."

"Show Vikram the projects exhibit."

"I will."

"We go to a children's hospital once a month."

"What do you do there?"

"Mostly we just talk or play a little bit. Some of the kids get really lonely."

EVERYONE MAKES A DIFFERENCE

"This is our multicultural project."

"What's that?"

"We learn about different cultures. Stories and language and stuff. What language do you speak in India?"

21

"There are lots of different languages in India. At home we speak Hindi and English."

"Neat. Maybe you can teach us some."

"Sure."

"What's that?"

"It's our citizenship project. We're building a park."

"Really? Kids are building a park?!"

"Kids, parents, everybody."

"Can my family join?"

"Sure."

"Hi, Miss Esparza. This is Vikram. He's from India. His family might join the park project."

"I'm glad we moved here."

"So are we, Vikram."

"You have really made us
feel at home."

28

WHAT DO YOU THINK?

Why did Matt and José say that it is dumb to throw litter?

IMPORTANT IDEAS

A sense of community – The good feeling that you have because you live in a place with other people.

On page 28, Vikram's parents say, "You have really made us feel at home."

What projects do you have at your school or in your community?

Now that you have read this book, see if you can answer these questions:

1. Who is Vikram and where does he come from?

2. What kinds of activities do Matt and José do at the Community Center?

3. What is the multicultural project?

4. What is the citizenship project?

5. How do the Hero Club kids participate in these events?

About the author

Cindy Leaney teaches English and writes books for both young readers and adults. She has lived and worked in England, Kenya, Mexico, Saudi Arabia, and the United States.

About the illustrator

Peter Wilks began work in advertising, where he developed a love for illustration. He has drawn pictures for many children's books in Great Britain and in the United States.

HERO CLUB CHARACTER VALUE SERIES

Everyone Makes a Difference (A Book About Community)

Field Trip (A Book About Sharing)

It's Your Turn Now (A Book About Politeness)

Lost and Found (A Book About Honesty)

Summer Vacation (A Book About Patience)

Taking Care of Mango (A Book About Responsibility)